Bobby _
Bad Day

Written by Julia Jarman
Illustrated by Julie Park

Chapter 1

'Come on, Jabeen!'
Mo called from the back of the bus.
'Come and sit with us.'
Mrs Hall's class were going on an outing.
They were going in a bus to a museum.
Some of the mums and dads were going too.

Mrs Hall called everybody's names,
'Sam?'
'Yes, Mrs Hall.'
'Jabeen?'
'Yes, Mrs Hall.'
'Tilak?'
'Yes, Mrs Hall.'
'Bobby?'
There was no answer.
Mrs Hall called Bobby's name again.
'Bobby? Where's Bobby?'
Again, there was no answer.

'Oh dear, Bobby isn't here,' said Mrs Hall.
'There's always one,' said the driver.

Then Sam shouted, 'Here he is! Here's Bobby!'
Bobby and his dad got on the bus.
Bobby's dad looked unhappy and so did Bobby.
'I want to sit at the back,' he said.
'You can't,' said his dad. 'Sit down here.'
The back seat was full.
'Sorry, Bobby,' said Mo.

Jabeen had a book about the museum.
Everybody on the back seat was looking at it.
'I want to see the mummies,' said Jabeen.
'So do I,' said Mo.
'I want to see the giant statues,' said Sam.
'I don't like museums,' said Bobby.
'I don't want to go.'
'Sit down,' said his dad, 'and don't be a pest.'
Bobby didn't look happy.

Soon, the driver started the bus and
Bobby's dad went to sleep.
Bobby started to eat his packed lunch.

Nobody saw him until
he was sick – in Tilak's cap.

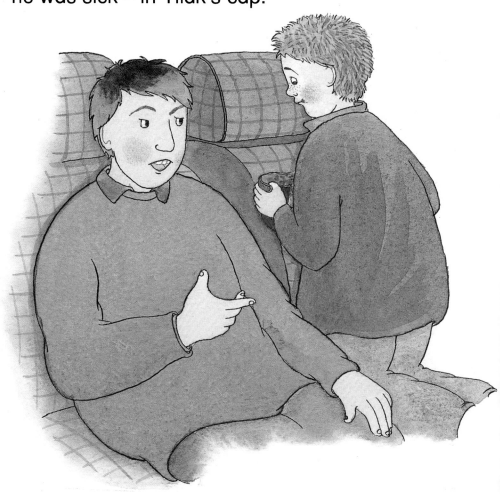

Bobby's dad woke up. He took one look at Bobby.
Then he looked at Tilak's cap.
'Oh, no!' he said.
'There's always one,' said the driver.

Chapter 2

They got to the museum and
the sun came out.
Everybody except Bobby ate their
packed lunches.
Bobby wasn't hungry and he still wasn't happy.
'What can I do?' he asked.
'You can wait for us,' said his dad,
'and try to cheer up.'

At last, they went into the museum and
Bobby started to look happy.
'Wow!' he said, 'Look at that.'
He was pointing to a giant with
wings and five legs.
There were lots of giants.
Tilak pointed to a giant's head.
'It's as big as a bus,' he said.
'It's great!' said Bobby.

Mo liked the cats. There were lots of cat statues.
Bobby liked the cats too.
'There's a mummy,' said Jabeen.
'Where's the daddy then?' said Bobby and
everybody laughed.

Then, a museum man came over.
He looked angry.
He pointed to a big letter B and said,
'What's this?'
There was no answer.
'Who did it?' asked the museum man.
There was still no answer but everybody
looked at Bobby.

'Oh Bobby!' said Mrs Hall.
'Oh dear!' said Bobby's dad.
'There's always one,' said the driver.
'It wasn't me,' said Bobby.
'B is for Bobby,' said the driver.

'It wasn't me!' shouted Bobby.
'Don't shout,' said the museum man.
'You can come with me.'
'I'll come too,' said Bobby's dad.
Mrs Hall was very upset.
'There's always one,' said the driver.

Mrs Hall took the other children to see
the mummies. She still looked upset.
The mummies were just like the
pictures in Jabeen's book, but Jabeen didn't
want to look at them now.
She was looking at a little girl.

Suddenly, she called out, 'Look, Mrs Hall. Look at that girl.'
Mrs Hall took one look.
Then, she ran towards the exit.

Chapter 3

Mrs Hall came back with the museum man,
and Bobby and his dad.
'There's the girl,' she said.
And she pointed to a girl with a big black pencil.

They all went over to the girl.
'What's your name little girl?'
asked the museum man.
'B. . .Belinda,' said the little girl.

'I said it wasn't me,' said Bobby.
'I'm sorry, Bobby,' said Mrs Hall.
The museum man said he was sorry too,
but the driver said nothing.
Then, Mrs Hall pointed to her watch.
'We must be going now,' she said.

'Do we have to?' asked Bobby.
'Can't we go to the museum shop?'
'All right,' said Mrs Hall. 'But we must be quick.'

They all went to the shop and
Mrs Hall bought a little cat statue for Bobby.
'I'm sorry, Bobby,' she said.

Bobby's dad bought
Tilak a new cap and
he bought Bobby a
mummy mask.

'You look after the mask, Dad,'
said Bobby.
'I just want to look at my
cat statue.'

Then, Mrs Hall said, 'Come on, everybody.
We must go back to the bus now.'

Jabeen bought a mummy mask and
so did Sam and Tilak.
Mo bought a little cat mummy.

They all went back to the bus.
Mrs Hall stopped and said, 'Is everybody here?'
'No!' Bobby said, 'My dad's not here!'
'He must be here,' said Mrs Hall.
'He must be on the bus.'

She got on the bus and called out,
'Mr Jones! Mr Jones!' There was no answer.
She got out. 'He's not there,' she said.
'Oh dear. What are we going to do?
We really must go now.'

'He must be in the museum,' said Jabeen's
mum and she went back to the museum to look.
Everybody waited.
Mrs Hall kept looking at her watch.

Soon, Jabeen's mum came back.
'He's not there,' she said.
'Oh dear,' said Mrs Hall, 'we have to go home.'
Everybody got on the bus.
Bobby was very upset.
'I was a pest,' he said. 'My dad was fed up
with me. And now he's gone.'
Sam gave him a sweet.
'You can sit on the back seat if you want,'
said Tilak.

'Oh, no, he can't,' said Sam, pointing
to the back seat.
'The back seat's full.'
Everybody looked.

'It's a mummy!' said Mo.
But Bobby said, 'That's not a mummy.
That's a daddy. It's my daddy!'
Then he laughed and shouted,
'Come on Dad! Wake up Dad!'

'There's always one,' said the driver.
And he started the bus.